# MY BIG BUMPER
# BOOK OF FUN

# EGMONT

*We bring stories to life*

**MR. MEN    LITTLE MISS**

MR. MEN™ LITTLE MISS™ © THOIP (a Sanrio company)

© 2012 THOIP (a Sanrio company)
Printed and published under licence from Price Stern Sloan, Inc., Los Angeles.
First published in Great Britain 2012 by Egmont UK Limited,
The Yellow Building, 1 Nicholas Road, London W11 4AN

ISBN 978 0 6035 6766 7
53062/1
Printed in Italy

# MY BIG BUMPER
# BOOK OF FUN

EGMONT

This book belongs to

..........................................

Mr. Silly

Mr. Greedy

# Meet the Mr. Men!

Mr. Funny

Mr. Tickle

Mr. Mischief

Mr. Messy

Mr. Small

Mr. Bump

Mr. Happy

Mr. Topsy-Turvy

Mr. Strong

# MR. TICKLE
## in a tangle

**Mr Tickle's long arms come in very handy - most of the time!**
**But imagine what trouble they cause when**
**they're not tickling!**

Now, who does that extraordinarily long arm belong to?

Of course! Mr Tickle.

And Mr Tickle's long, long arms come in very handy.

They can reach kites caught in trees.

They can answer the phone when Mr Tickle is in the bath.

But, most importantly, they are splendidly perfect for tickling!

Tickling people round corners.

Tickling people through upstairs windows.

And even tickling people on the other side of letter boxes!

However, there are days when those extraordinarily long arms are not so handy.

Days when they are nothing but a nuisance.

Days like last Monday.

Mr Tickle was lying in bed eating breakfast when he heard his garden gate open. It was Mr Stamp, the postman.

Quick as a flash Mr Tickle sent one of his long arms down the stairs to tickle Mr Stamp.

Or, that is what he intended to do, but somehow or other, his arm got tangled up in the banisters.

Poor Mr Tickle!

It took him an hour to untangle his arm!

The letter Mr Stamp had delivered was an invitation from Mr Uppity, for lunch at the Grand Hotel.

Mr Tickle took the bus to town and sat on the upper deck.

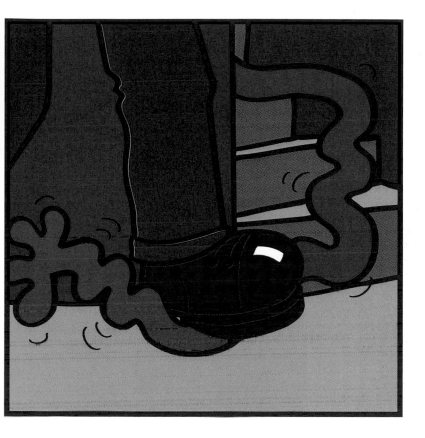

Mr Tickle sent one of his long arms down the stairs to tickle the bus driver, but, somehow or other, the ticket inspector trod on his arm!

OUCH!

Mr Tickle arrived at the Grand Hotel and rushed through the revolving door.

Or rather he tried to, but, somehow or other, his arms caught in the door.

The fire brigade had to be called out to untangle his arms, by which time he had missed lunch.

Poor Mr Tickle.

No lunch, and even worse, no tickles!

It was a very sad Mr Tickle who set off for home.

Suddenly he heard something.

He stopped. Somebody was approaching from around the corner.

Mr Tickle smiled to himself.

And sent both his arms around the corner to tickle that somebody.

But that somebody was Little Miss Naughty.

And she tied those extraordinarily long arms together in a knot!

When he got home Mr Tickle fell back into his armchair.

What a terrible day. Not one tickle!

Suddenly there was a knock at the door.

It was Little Miss Tiny.

Mr Tickle stretched out one of his extraordinarily long arms.

Well, one tickle was better than none.

Even if it was only a tiny tickle!

Mr Tickle has picked a bunch of pretty flowers. Colour in
all the buzzing bees using your yellow crayon.

Whoops! Mr Bump has been covered in yellow paint.
Colour him in, adding in extra paint splashes, too!

Mr Nosey would like to fly the box-shaped kite.
Colour it in using your red crayon.

"Atishoo!" Mr Sneeze has blown Mr Bounce into a plant pot!
Colour in the flowers using your favourite crayons.

**Mr Strong works out by carrying Mr Greedy when cleaning.
Add some more heavy things to the scene.**

**Can you guess what Little Miss Sunshine is holding?**
**Draw a picture of the gift.**

Mr Funny has played a joke on Mr Grumpy! Make this scene really colourful using your favourite crayons.

Mr Clever lives in Cleverland. His favourite hobby is reading.
Colour in the books as neatly as you can.

Mr Chatterbox just won't stop talking – even when he should be driving the bus! Colour in his unhappy passengers.

# MR. SILLY
## gets the giggles

**Lots of silly things happen in Nonsenseland.**

**So what could possibly give Mr Silly the giggles?**

Mr Silly lives in a place
called Nonsenseland
where the grass is blue
and the trees are red.
Which you already know.

It is also a place where
zebra crossings are
spotty. Which you
probably did not know.

In Nonsenseland you post
letters in telephone boxes
and you make phone calls
from letter boxes.

And in Nonsenseland the umbrellas all have holes in them so that you know when it has stopped raining.

Which is utter nonsense, but not if your name is Mr Silly.

Now, one morning last week, Mr Silly got up, put on his hat, brushed his teeth with soap, as usual, polished his shoes with toothpaste, as usual, and went down to breakfast.

For breakfast, Mr Silly had fried eggs and custard, as usual, and a cup of hot, milky marmalade, as usual.

After breakfast he went out into his garden. The day before Mr Silly had bought a tree, but as he looked at the tree he realised that he did not have a hole to plant it in.

So he went to the hardware shop.

"Good morning," said Mr Silly. "I would like to buy a hole."

"Sorry," said the sales assistant, "we're all out of holes. Sold the last one yesterday."

"Bother," said Mr Silly.

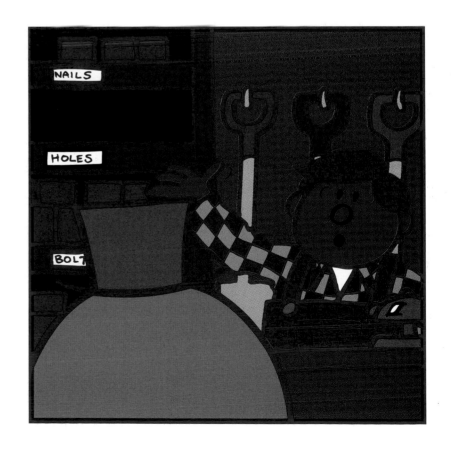

He decided there was
nothing for it but to go in
search of a hole.
He walked and he walked
and he walked.
Eventually Mr Silly stopped
walking and looked down
at his feet.
"That's odd," he said,
"this grass is green."

"Of course it is," said a
voice behind him. "Grass is
always green."
"Who are you?" asked
Mr Silly.
"Little Miss Wise."
"I'm Mr Silly. Could you
tell me where I am?"
"You're in Sensibleland,"
said Miss Wise.

Mr Silly had walked so far that he had walked right out of
Nonsenseland.

"I'm looking for a hardware shop," said Mr Silly. "Can you help?"

"Certainly," said Miss Wise. "Follow me."

As they walked along Mr Silly looked around.

He had never seen anywhere like it. The grass was green,

the trees were green, even the hedges were green.

They came to a zebra crossing. A stripy zebra crossing.

Mr Silly chuckled, and then he giggled and then he laughed out loud.

"Why are you laughing?" asked Miss Wise.

"The ... hee hee ... zebra crossing ... ha ha ... is stripy," laughed Mr Silly.

"What else would a zebra crossing be?" said Miss Wise.

"Spotty, of course!" said Mr Silly, wiping the tears from his eyes.

"How silly," said Miss Wise.

They set off again and the further they went the more Mr Silly laughed.

He laughed when he saw someone posting a letter in a letter box.

He laughed when he saw someone using a phone in a telephone box.

He laughed when he saw an umbrella without holes in it.

Eventually they came to Miss Bolt's Hardware Shop.

"Good afternoon," said Mr Silly. "I would like to buy a hole."

"A hole?" questioned Miss Bolt.

"Yes, big enough to plant a tree in," explained Mr Silly.

Miss Bolt sniggered. Miss Wise chortled.

And then they burst out laughing.

"I've never heard anything so absurd," laughed Miss Bolt.

"But I do have something that may help."

That evening Mr Silly invited his friend Mr Nonsense for supper
and told him all about his day in Sensibleland.

Mr Nonsense laughed so hard he fell off his chair!

"... and then," continued Mr Silly, "Miss Privet gave me a spade.
A spade! Why in the world would I want to buy a spade when
all I wanted was a hole!"

"Hee hee ... that's ... ha ha ... ridiculous!" laughed Mr Nonsense.
"What's for pudding?"

"Spam roly-poly," answered Mr Silly.

"Oh, goody," said Mr Nonsense. "My favourite."

**What is Mr Silly using as a fishing rod?**
**Colour in the scene as neatly as you can.**

**Little Miss Birthday really loves going to parties!**
**Draw two colourful balloons for her to hold.**

Colour in this mischievous scene as neatly as you can.
Can you name all the characters?

Mr Mean has lost all his money and is very unhappy!
Colour the clouds in grey to suit his mood.

**Mr Greedy is on the hunt for something good to eat.
Can you draw him a tasty snack?**

# MR. BUMP
## loses his memory

**This time Mr Bump has bumped his head once
too often! Find out what happens when he
starts to believe he is really Mr Careful!**

Mr Bump is the sort of person who is always having accidents.

Small accidents.

Medium-sized accidents.

And big accidents.

Lots and lots
of accidents.

One day Mr Bump got out of bed, or rather, he fell out of bed, as he did every morning.

He drew back the curtains and opened the window.

It was a beautiful day.

He leant on the windowsill and breathed in deeply and ...

fell out of the window.

BUMP!

Mr Bump sat up and rubbed his head. And as he rubbed, it dawned on him that he had no idea where he was.

He had no idea whose garden he was sitting in.

He had no idea whose house he was sitting in front of.

And he had no idea who he was.

Mr Bump had lost his memory.

Mr Bump walked up to his garden gate and looked down the lane.
Mr Muddle was passing by. "Good afternoon," said Mr Muddle.
As you and I know, it was morning. But Mr Muddle, not
surprisingly, always gets things in a muddle.

"I seem to have lost my memory," said Mr Bump. "Do you know
what my name is?"

"You're Mr Careful," said Mr Muddle.

"Thank you," said Mr Bump.

Mr Bump went into town. The first person he met was Mrs Packet the grocer, carrying an armful of groceries.

"Hello," said Mr Bump, "I'm Mr Careful, can I help?"

"Just the person! I need someone careful to deliver these eggs."

Mr Bump took the eggs from Mrs Packet and set off down the High Street.

And because he was Mr Bump he slipped and fell on the eggs, breaking all of them.

"You're not all that careful, are you?" said Mrs Packet.

"Sorry," said Mr Bump.

He walked on past the dairy. Mr Bottle, the manager, came out.

"I'm looking for someone to drive the milk float," he said. "What's your name?"

"Mr Careful," replied Mr Bump.

"Perfect," said Mr Bottle. "I need someone careful to do the milk round."

Mr Bump set off down the road.

As he rounded the corner he hit the kerb and the milk float turned over, smashing all the milk bottles.

"Well, that wasn't very carefully done, was it?" said Mr Bottle.

"Sorry," said Mr Bump.

Then he met Mr Brush, the painter, who was up a ladder, painting.

"Hello," said Mr Bump. "I'm Mr Careful. Do you need a hand?"

"Yes, please," replied Mr Brush. "I need someone careful to pass up that paint pot."

Mr Bump began to climb the ladder.

And being Mr Bump, he fell off and the pot of paint landed on his head.

Mr Bump went for a walk.

"I don't understand it," he said to himself. "My name is

Mr Careful, but I can't do anything carefully!"

It was then that he walked into a tree.

BUMP!

And bumped his head.

An apple fell out of the tree into his hand.

"That's odd," he said to himself. "How did I get here?

The last thing I remember is opening my bedroom window."

"... And where did all this paint come from?"

You know, don't you.

Just at that moment Farmer Fields turned up.

"Careful ..." he called.

"That sounds familiar," said Mr Bump,
and fell down the bank into the river.

Mr Bump is bouncing a ball – boing!
Colour it in using your yellow and green crayons.

**Poor Mr Rush is in such a hurry, he hasn't spotted the banana skin!
Colour him in using your purple crayon.**

Mr Messy is having so much fun splashing around,
he has lost his umbrella. Can you draw him one?

**Mr Sneeze has a bad cold. Colour him in using your crayons – make sure his nose is red!**

**Little Miss Naughty is up to her usual tricks!**
**Count the spiders then colour in the scene.**

# MR. FUNNY
## upsets Mr. Fussy

**Mr Funny can always make people laugh.
But when he makes Mr Fussy laugh,
he causes all kinds of trouble!**

Mr Funny lives in a teapot-shaped house.

He drives a shoe-shaped car.

And he has a teacup-shaped bath.

Mr Fussy lives in a very ordinary house, drives a very ordinary car and his bath is a very ordinary bath.

Mr Funny is a very funny fellow.

So funny that when he pulls one of his funny faces you can't help but laugh.

Mr Fussy is very serious.

Very serious about keeping everything neat and tidy and spick and span.

Now Mr Funny lives at the very end of Long Lane and Mr Fussy lives half-way down Long Lane.

So whenever Mr Funny goes out for a drive in his shoe car he has to pass Mr Fussy's house.

Every time that Mr Funny passes Mr Fussy he pulls one of his funny faces.

And as hard as he tries, Mr Fussy can't help laughing.

He laughs so much that he ends up having accidents.

Like the time he was mowing his lawn.

He laughed so much he ruined all his nice straight lines.

And when he was cleaning his windows.

He laughed so much he fell off his ladder and squashed his prize pumpkin.

And he burnt his shoelaces while he was ironing them.

Mr Fussy was fed up.

But then he had an idea.

He put up a sign on the lane just before his house.

It read: 'Please Beep Your Horn.'

"That should work," he said to himself.

The idea was that if Mr Funny beeped his horn Mr Fussy would have some warning and he could stop whatever it was he was doing.

The next day Mr Funny was driving down the lane as usual when he saw Mr Fussy's sign.

So he beeped his car's horn.

Now, so far Mr Fussy's idea had worked, but what he had not reckoned on was the sound that Mr Funny's car horn would make.

It doesn't go 'BEEP.'

Oh no, it sounds like somebody making a very loud raspberry noise.

'THURRRPT!' went the car horn.

Mr Fussy was outside in his coal bunker. Stacking his coal in neat rows. Mr Fussy didn't like untidy piles of coal!

When Mr Fussy heard the sound Mr Funny's car horn made, he started to giggle.

And then he chuckled. And then he laughed.

And he laughed so much he fell over into his neatly stacked coal.

Once he had recovered from his laughing fit he stormed out of his coal bunker.

He was covered from head to foot in coal.

And he was furious. He stormed over to Mr Funny.

"That's the most ridiculous car horn I've ever heard," he yelled at Mr Funny.

Mr Funny stopped his shoe car beside Mr Fussy's gate.

"There's a reason for that," he explained. "It's because it's not a car horn, it's a ..."

" ... shoe-horn, ha ha ha, hee hee hee," he laughed.

And even Mr Fussy had to admit that was quite funny.

Wouldn't you agree?

Choo! Choo! Jump aboard Mr Funny's train.
Colour it in using your brightest crayons.

Mr Happy is very excited – he is going to Mr Nosey's birthday party!
Draw two more balloons for Mr Happy to take.

Mr Nosey is going exploring under the sea.
Can you count all of the fish?

**Who is Mr Happy talking to on the telephone?**
**Colour him in as neatly as you can.**

**Mr Birthday has baked a birthday cake for Mr Nosey.
Count the candles then colour it in.**

# MR. GREEDY
## is helpfully heavy

**Mr Greedy is getting heavier and heavier which
is quite a problem - until he finds a way
to put his weight to work!**

Mr Greedy likes to eat.

And the more he eats the bigger he gets and the bigger he gets the heavier he becomes.

Which was a problem, as you will see.

Mr Greedy woke up and yawned and stretched.

CRACK!

BUMP!

The 'CRACK!' was the sound of Mr Greedy's bed breaking and the 'BUMP!' was the sound of Mr Greedy hitting the floor.

"Oh dear," said Mr Greedy.

Mr Greedy got up off the floor and went into the bathroom and ran a bath.
But when he got into the bath all the water got out.
There was not enough room in the bath for both Mr Greedy and the water!

"Oh dear," he said again. Mr Greedy looked at himself in his mirror.

He had a wide mirror, but he was even wider and could not see very much of himself.

"Oh dear."

He went downstairs for breakfast.

As he waited for the bread to toast he let his hand rest on the loaf of bread.

And squashed it flat.

He even had heavy hands!

After a large breakfast of squashed toast he leant back in his chair.
There was another loud 'CRACK!' and 'BUMP!'
He found himself on the floor again.
"I wish I wasn't so heavy," he sighed to himself.

Now Mr Greedy had been invited to Mr Uppity's house for lunch.

So Mr Greedy squeezed through his front door and squeezed into his car. He started the engine.

Then, with four loud bangs, all four tyres on his car burst.

BANG! BANG! BANG! BANG!

He had to get the bus.

But when he climbed on, the other end of the bus tipped up!

"I think you need to lose some weight," suggested the

bus conductor.

As the bus drove off without him, Mr Greedy looked down at his large tummy.

"Oh dear," he sighed, not for the first time that day.

Mr Greedy had to walk all the way to Mr Uppity's house. He was very tired and very hot and very hungry when he got there.

Mr Uppity lived in the biggest house in Bigtown. Mr Uppity was very rich.

Mr Uppity answered the door.

"What do you want?" he demanded.

Mr Uppity was very rude.

"You invited me for lunch," said Mr Greedy.

"Oh yes," said Mr Uppity. "You'll have to wait. I'm very busy."

"What are you doing?" asked Mr Greedy.

"Packing," answered Mr Uppity, and went up to his bedroom.

Mr Greedy followed.

Mr Uppity's bedroom was full of suitcases and every suitcase was overflowing. Mr Uppity went round the room trying to close them, but they were so full it was impossible.

"Don't just stand there, give me a hand," ordered Mr Uppity bossily.

Mr Greedy tried pushing a suitcase shut, but it was no good.

Then he had an idea.

He sat on the lid of the suitcase, and because he was so heavy the suitcase closed.

"Brilliant," said Mr Uppity.
"You can shut the rest."

Mr Greedy beamed.

For the first time in a very long time Mr Greedy had found something useful that he could do.

and they all lived happily every after. The End.

Going on Holiday?
Having trouble fitting everything in your suitcase?
**Then call**
**Mr. Greedy.**
The expert suitcase squasher.

holiday to the g
when he return
said what a lov
Disaster strikes
the daisy above
Small's house i
blown over in h
winds.

Mr. Strong brea
eating record b
eggs. Ask how
he said 'very str

Little Miss Bos
fell over laughi
which is very u

And on his way home Mr Greedy had an idea.

An idea that meant he could be useful every day.

He went to the local newspaper and placed an advertisement.

Mr Greedy had found himself a job.

He went home, ate a huge supper to celebrate, went to bed
and slept.

And do you know how he slept? I'll tell you.

He slept ...

... heavily.

**Mr Tickle loves to tickle all his friends!**
**Colour him in using your orange crayon.**

Mr Silly is having tea with Mr Nonsense.
Colour in the funny scene.

Mr Noisy has tried everything to wake up Mr Lazy but he won't budge!
Make Mr Lazy's quilt as bright and colourful as you can.

**Little Miss Naughty loves getting up to mischief!**
**Colour in her umbrella using your pink crayon.**

Mr Forgetful has been gardening but he can't remember
where he's left his tools! Colour in the scene.

# MR. STRONG
## and the flood

**Mr Strong is beginning to wish he wasn't quite so strong -
until he comes across a farmer in need of help!**

Mr Strong is unbelievably strong.

So strong that sometimes he forgets his own strength.

Like the other day.

It was raining.

So Mr Strong pulled on his wellington boots. But he pulled too hard and his foot went right through the bottom of his boot!

Then he went out
through his front door
and opened his umbrella.

But he pushed too hard
and turned the umbrella
inside out!

So he tried to go back inside
to get another umbrella
(Mr Strong gets through a
lot of umbrellas) but when
he turned the doorknob it
came off in his hand.

Poor Mr Strong was not
having a good day.

Fortunately, when you are as strong as Mr Strong you don't need a door to get inside your house.

Do you know what he did?

He picked up the corner of his house and slipped in under the wall!

Once he had fetched a new umbrella and opened it (very carefully this time) and opened his door (very carefully) he set off for his walk.

Now, as you might remember, I mentioned that it was raining. What I did not tell you was that it had been raining for days and days and days. Nearly a whole week. Non-stop!

The river in the valley below Mr Strong's house had burst its banks and was flooding the meadows.

Mr Strong walked down the lane beneath the dripping trees.

It was not long before he met a very worried looking Farmer Fields.

"Good morning," said Mr Strong. "What's the matter?"

"It's my sheep," said Farmer Fields. "They're stuck in the meadow surrounded by water. I can't get them out!"

"Let's go and see," said Mr Strong. "I might be able to help."

Poor Farmer Fields' sheep were indeed in trouble.

And the bit of dry land left for them to stand on was getting smaller by the minute as the flood water rose higher.

Mr Strong waded out to the little island in the middle of the meadow and then waded back carrying two sheep above his head. "Oh, well done," said Farmer Fields. "The only problem is that there are ninety-eight sheep left out there and we'll run out of time before you've carried them all across!"

"Mmmm," said Mr Strong. "I fear you may be right, but I think I have an idea. Do you mind if I borrow your barn?"

Farmer Fields smiled.

And you are probably smiling if you have read the other story about Mr Strong.

But for those of you who have not read that Mr Strong story, I'll tell you what he did.

He picked up the barn (that's right, a whole barn!) and carried it across to the sheep.

Then he lifted all the sheep into the barn, counting them carefully as he did, so as not to leave any behind.

And then he picked up the barn with all ninety-eight sheep inside, and waded back to Farmer Fields.

"Oh, thank you," said Farmer Fields, once all his sheep were safely in the field at the top of the hill.

"Barns are very handy things to have lying around," chuckled Mr Strong, and went home.

That evening Mr Strong ate an enormous plateful of fried eggs and went to bed early ...

... and fell fast ASHEEP! HA! HA!

**Mr Strong is the strongest person in the whole wide world.
Colour him in using your red crayon.**

**Colour in Mr Greedy. Can you think of any
other food he might like to eat?**

**The Little Misses are making music together! Can you name any of the instruments they are playing?**

Once Mr Chatterbox starts talking, he can go on for hours!
Colour in Mr Chatterbox using your pink crayon.

Mr Strong has gone to the farm to buy some eggs.
Colour in the farmyard scene.

# MR. TOPSY-TURVY
## the round way wrong

Mr Topsy-Turvy likes doing things the wrong
way round - so imagine what happens
when he decides to move house!

If Mr Topsy-Turvy can do something the wrong way round then you can be certain that he will.

Like the way he drives a car.

Which explains why you never see him driving a car... and why he travels by bus.

Mr Topsy-Turvy woke up early one morning.

He has a very topsy-turvy way of sleeping in bed, as you can see.

He yawned and stretched and got up.

Then he went upstairs
for breakfast.

That's right, Mr Topsy-Turvy's
house is just as topsy-turvy
as he is.

All his bedrooms are downstairs
and his kitchen and living room
are upstairs.

Mr Topsy-Turvy decided to have
cornflakes for breakfast.
He opened the packet.
But being Mr Topsy-Turvy
he didn't pour the cornflakes
out, oh no, he poured the
milk into the packet!
His meals tend to be
very messy affairs.

After he had finished breakfast Mr Topsy-Turvy caught the bus into town.

"One town for ticket, please," he said to the bus driver.

The bus driver scratched his head.

"Don't you mean, one ticket for town?" he said.

"Right that's," said Mr Topsy-Turvy.

Mr Topsy-Turvy speaks as topsy-turvily as everything else he does.

Now, this day was a rather special day for Mr Topsy-Turvy.

He had been saving up to buy a new house.

He went into Mr Homes' estate agency and said, "I'd like new to house a buy."

Mr Homes knew Mr Topsy-Turvy quite well.

"You mean, you'd like to buy a new house?"

"Right that's," said Mr Topsy-Turvy, for the second time that day.

"If you wait outside the front I'll go and get my car," said Mr Homes.

And of course Mr Topsy-Turvy waited outside the back.

After Mr Homes eventually found him they set off in the car to look at some houses.

They looked at all sorts.

Tall, skinny houses.

Short, squat houses.

Even short, skinny houses, but Mr Topsy-Turvy didn't like any of them.

None of them seemed quite right to him.

As they were driving back to town Mr Topsy-Turvy suddenly shouted to Mr Homes to stop the car.

Well, what he actually said was, "Stop car the!" but Mr Homes knew what he meant.

On the other side of a hedge was the strangest house you have ever seen.

Everything was upside-down. In fact, everything was topsy-turvy.

And I'm sure you can guess whose house it was.

"Now, house of that's the sort want I," said Mr Topsy-Turvy.

"But ..." said Mr Homes, "but that's your house!"

"Right that's," said Mr Topsy-Turvy, for the third time that day.

"But you can't move house into your own house!" exclaimed
Mr Homes. "That would be all the round way wrong ... I mean
the wrong way round."

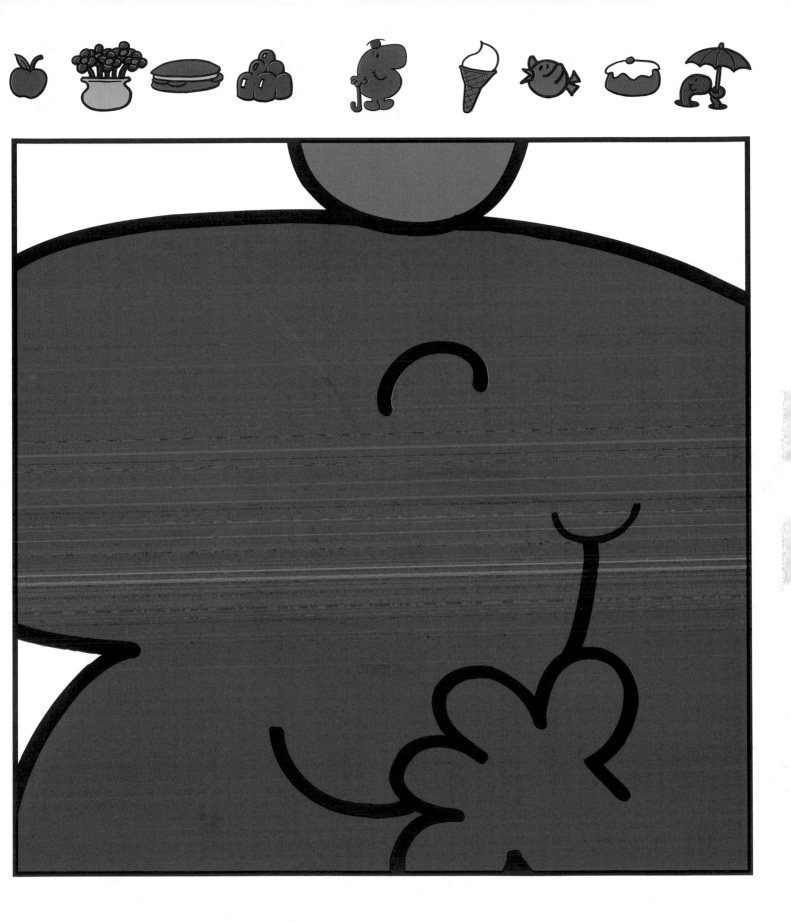

Mr Topsy-Turvy grinned a huge grin.

"Exactly," he said.

Oh dear! Mr Topsy-Turvy has got muddled again.
Colour him in using your orange crayon.

**Poor Mr Clumsy has fallen over again!**
**Colour him in as neatly as you can.**

Mr Messy and Mr Silly are off for a walk in the countryside.
Can you add some silly things to the scene?

**Colour in Little Miss Greedy's cupcakes,
then add some more sugary snacks.**

Colour in the balloons as brightly as you can.
Why not draw on patterns, too?

# MR. SMALL
# a big day out

**Mr Small is really very small indeed.**

**Imagine what would happen if Mr Small**

**suddenly became very big!**

Mr Small was out for a walk.

He was feeling more than a little sorry
for himself.

It wasn't much fun being as small as he was.

He sat down under a tree and closed his eyes.
"I do so wish I was bigger," he sighed.

"Much, much bigger," he added.

Now, Mr Small did not know that there was a wizard lying down on the other side of the tree.

He had stopped for a snooze and, just as he had been dozing off, the wizard had overheard Mr Small's wish.

The wizard smiled to himself.

Without even opening his eyes, he muttered some magic words under his breath and then went back to sleep.

As Mr Small lay there, something really quite remarkable happened.

Something really quite remarkably magic.

Mr Small began to grow.

And grow.

And grow.

Until he bumped his head on a branch!

When he crawled out from underneath the tree and stood up he was taller than the tree. Much taller.

"Gosh," said Mr Small. He could not believe his eyes.

He could not believe his size!

He went for a walk to try out his new size.

It was wonderful.

He could see over the top of everything.

He leap-frogged over trees and jumped over rivers.

He gave Mr Uppity the shock of his life.

He was stronger than Mr Strong.

Noisier than Mr Noisy.

And taller than Mr Tall!

He could even make his fingers meet when he put his arms around Mr Greedy's tummy!

Mr Small had a marvellous day, and as the sun set he lay down in a field and went to sleep.

As Mr Small slept he shrank back to his normal size.

For you see, the wizard had only cast a spell that would last one day.

When Mr Small woke up it was dark.

"What a wonderful dream," he said to himself, and got up
to walk home.

But he found he couldn't. He was surrounded by a wall!
However, when he felt along the bottom, he discovered that
he could lift up the wall.

It was light outside, and when he crawled out Mr Small could
not believe his eyes.

He had been trapped underneath a hat!

A hat that looked just like his own, but it was much, much bigger.

"Well, I never," said Mr Small. "Maybe it wasn't a dream after all."

That sleepy old wizard had forgotten to finish off his spell properly.

He had forgotten to make sure Mr Small's hat had shrunk back to the right size.

Mr Small now had a ten-gallon hat.

A ten-gallon hat for a pint-sized person!

**Mr Small is keeping out of the rain! Decorate his umbrella using your favourite crayons.**

Boom! Mr Noisy loves banging his drum very loudly.
Draw another instrument for him to play.

**Which Mr Men can you see in the picture?**
**Colour them in as brightly as you can.**

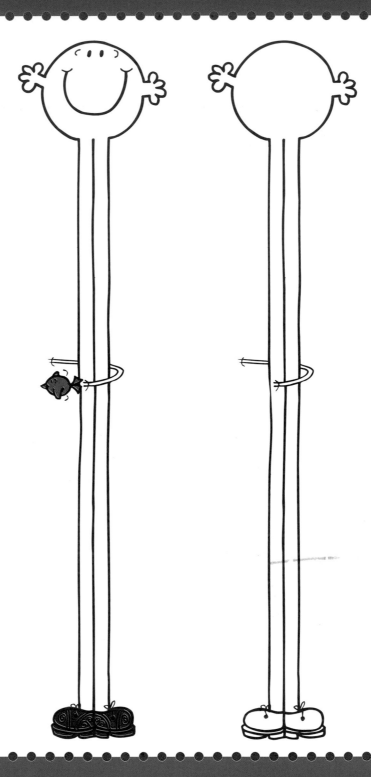

**Finish the second picture of Mr Tall
by drawing in the missing details.**

**Draw something funny for Mr Tickle to watch on television, using your crayons.**

# MR. MISCHIEF
## a spot of trouble

**Mr Mischief thinks he has found the perfect
new way of spreading some mischief!
But has he?**

Mr Mischief woke up and groaned.

He did not feel well.

In fact, he felt decidedly unwell.

He got up and went to the bathroom to look at himself in the mirror.

He was covered in spots!

So he made an appointment with Dr Makeyouwell.

"You've got measles," said the doctor, "and the best thing you can do is go home to bed and stay there for a week."

Mr Mischief's face fell. A whole week in bed.

No mischief for a whole week!

Mr Mischief groaned for the second time that day.

"And don't forget," said Dr Makeyouwell as Mr Mischief was leaving, "measles are very catching."

Mr Mischief closed the door and then he grinned.

A very mischievous grin.

The sort of grin that meant that he was about to get up to no good.

Before he went home, Mr Mischief popped into the hardware shop and bought a pot of yellow paint.

Then he painted over all his spots, before paying Mr Happy a visit.

He didn't stay long, just long enough.

Long enough, thought Mr Mischief as he walked home, to give Mr Happy the measles!

When he got home he went to bed and lay there chuckling to himself. What a nasty person he is!

All the next day he lay in bed and thought about the trick he had played on Mr Happy.

And he thought, if Mr Happy had the measles, then Mr Tickle might catch them from Mr Happy.

Mr Mischief chuckled at the thought of Mr Tickle with spots all over his long arms.

And Mr Nosey might catch the measles from Mr Tickle.

And he chuckled at the thought of Mr Nosey with a spotty nose.

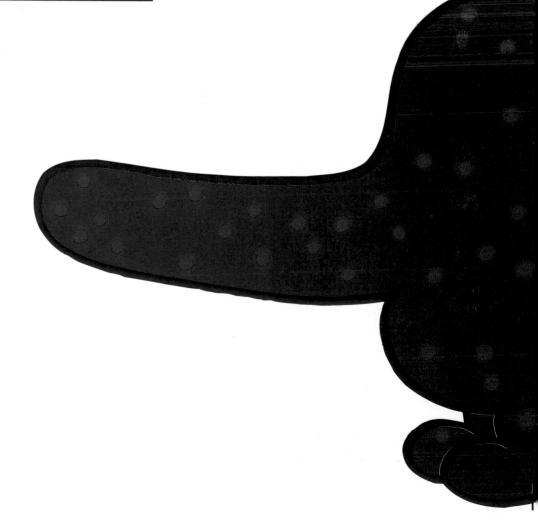

And he chuckled at the thought
of Mr Tall with spotty legs.

And Mr Wrong, who would probably
have blue spots, because he gets
everything wrong.

And Little Miss Tiny would only have room for one spot on her body.

"This will keep me happy all week long," chuckled Mr Mischief to himself.

Just then there was a knock at the door.

Mr Mischief struggled out of bed and answered it.

"Hello," said Mr Happy. "I heard you had the measles so I thought I'd come round and cheer you up. Here, I bought you these."

Mr Happy gave Mr Mischief a bunch of grapes.

Mr Mischief looked at Mr Happy, but as hard he looked, he couldn't see any spots. Not one!

"Aren't you afraid of catching the measles from me?"
stammered Mr Mischief.

"Of course not," said Mr Happy. "I've already had them.
And as you know, you can only get measles once!"

Mr Mischief's face fell and he groaned.

Again.

"What's wrong?" asked Mr Happy.

"Don't you like grapes?"

Mr Happy is enjoying his afternoon tea. Make him even happier by drawing him a picture for his wall.

Mr Uppity loves to count up all his money.
How many money bags can you see?

The Mr. Men are having lots of fun at the zoo!
Can you name all the animals in the scene?

Oh no! Little Miss Naughty is being bad again!
Colour in her scooter as neatly as you can.

**Poor Mr Bump has slipped up in a puddle!**
**Colour in his umbrella to cheer him up.**

# MR. MESSY
# messing about
# in the snow

**Mr Messy is the messiest person you
are ever likely to meet. Find out how
messy he can get when it snows!**

Mr Messy is the messiest person you are ever likely to meet.

He never has a bath.

His bathtub is full of cobwebs.

And his windows are so dirty he can't see out of them.

Which is why it was two days before he realised that it had snowed.

Mr Messy's garden is normally the messiest in the street.

Unlike the garden next door.

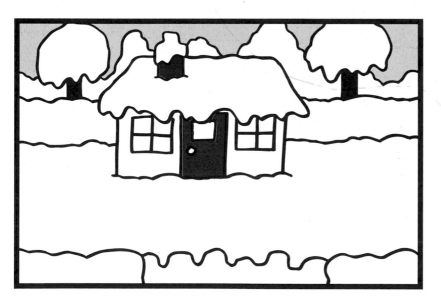

But now, with a covering of snow, you couldn't tell them apart.

Mr Messy went outside and promptly tripped over a rake hidden under the snow.

A rake that had been lying there for three years!

He walked down to his shed at the bottom of his garden.

A shed so full of odds and ends and bits and bobs that the door would not shut.

Mr Messy knew that underneath all that rubbish there was a toboggan.

So he pulled out all the odds and ends and bits and bobs, until eventually he found his toboggan at the back of the shed.

And then do you think
Mr Messy put everything
back in the shed?

Don't be silly!

Messy old Mr Messy.

Mr Messy spent the rest of the
day playing in the snow.

He tobogganed, and he
threw snowballs, and
he made snowmen.

He had the best, and busiest, day that he could
remember for a long time.

But there was one thing that made it even better.

Something that he enjoyed best of all. Being messy!

You see, Mr Messy is
so grubby that whatever
he touches he makes
as grubby and as messy
as he is.

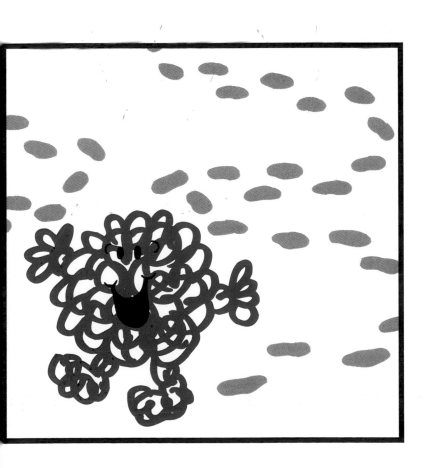

Everywhere he went he
left messy footprints.

And messy toboggan marks.

And messy snowballs.

And even messy snowmen.

By the end of the day Mr Messy's garden was once again
the messiest in the street.

Mr Messy went indoors a happy man, and wiped his feet ...

... on the carpet!

**Watch out for Mr Tickle, Mr Messy! Add a fun background to the picture then colour everything in.**

Mr Grumpy is in a very bad mood indeed.
Colour him using your blue crayon.

Mr Tickle has taken Mr Bump by surprise!
Colour them both in as neatly as you can.

Mr Birthday and Little Miss Birthday are celebrating!
Whose birthday is it?

**Silly Mr Messy is floating away on a party balloon!**
**Colour in the scene as neatly as you can.**

# MR. HAPPY
## finds a hobby

**Lots of the Mr Men have hobbies.
But do you think Mr Happy can find
the right hobby for Mr Grumble?**

Mr Happy is a happy sort of fellow.

He lives in Happyland which is a happy sort of place.

Behind his house there is a wood full of happy birds and on the other side of the wood there is a lake full of happy fish.

Now, one day, not that long ago, Mr Happy went for a walk down through the wood.

As he came to the shore of the lake he heard an unusual sound.

A sound that is seldom heard in Happyland. It was the sound of somebody moaning and grumbling.

Mr Happy peered round the trunk of a tree.

At the edge of the lake there was somebody fishing.

Fishing and grumbling.

And grumbling and fishing.

It was Mr Grumble.

"Good morning, Mr Grumble," said Mr Happy.

"Ssssh!" ssshed Mr Grumble.

"Sorry," whispered Mr Happy. "Have you caught anything?"

"Yes! I've caught a cold!" grumbled Mr Grumble. "I've been sitting here all night. I hate fishing!"

"Then, why *are* you fishing?" asked Mr Happy.

"Because Mr Quiet said it was fun! And, you see I'm trying to find something I enjoy doing. Something I can do as a hobby."

"Hmmm," pondered Mr Happy. "I might be able to help.
Come on, let's see if we can find you a hobby."
As they walked along, Mr Happy thought long and hard,
and as he thought, Mr Grumble grumbled.
He grumbled about the noise the birds were making.
He grumbled about having to walk.
But most of all he grumbled about not having a hobby.
Grumble, grumble, grumble.

First of all they met Mr Rush in his car. Mr Happy explained
what they were doing.
"What's your hobby?" asked Mr Grumble.
"Speed!" said Mr Rush. "Hop in!"
And they did. Mr Grumble very quickly decided that he did
not like going fast.

Next they met Little Miss Giggles.

"What's your hobby?" asked Mr Grumble.

"I...tee hee...like...tee hee...giggling," giggled Miss Giggles.

So they went to the circus to see the clowns.

Little Miss Giggles giggled, Mr Happy laughed and Mr Grumble...

frowned!

"I hate custard pies," grumbled Mr Grumble.

It proved to be a very
long day for Mr Happy.

They went everywhere.

They went to Little
Miss Splendid's house.

But Mr Grumble did not
like hats.

They went to Mr Mischief's
house.

But Mr Grumble did
not like practical jokes.

They bounced with Mr Bounce.

And looked through
keyholes with Mr Nosey.

But nothing was right.
In fact nothing was left.

Mr Happy had run out
of ideas.

As the sun was setting
they saw Mr Impossible
coming towards them
down the lane.

"Now, if anybody can help us that somebody ought to be Mr Impossible," said Mr Happy.

"Hello," he said. "You're good at the impossible. Can you think of a hobby that Mr Grumble would enjoy?"

"That..." said Mr Impossible.

"Yes..." said Mr Happy and Mr Grumble together.

"...would be impossible," said Mr Impossible.

"Grrr!" growled Mr Grumble, and stomped off home.

It was whilst drinking a cup of tea the next morning that Mr Happy had an idea.

A perfectly obvious idea.

He rushed round to Mr Grumble's house.

"I've got it!" cried Mr Happy. "You can take up fishing."

"Fishing!? But I hate fishing."

"I know, but what do you do while you are fishing?" asked Mr Happy.

"I don't know."

"You grumble," said Mr Happy.

"And what do you like doing most of all?"

"I like..." and then it dawned on Mr Grumble. "I like grumbling!" Mr Grumble looked at Mr Happy and then, for the first time in a very long time he smiled.

A very small smile, but a smile all the same.

THE END